Louisa M. Alcott

LITTLE WOMEN

ANDRE DEUTSCH ILLUSTRATED CLASSICS

IN THE DAYS OF "LITTLE WOMEN"...

Dresses in the late 1800s were long, and often decorated with bows and ruffles.

Carriages of that period.

This is how the men dressed.

The padding was called a "bustle".

Every-day clothes.

Riding clothes.

Corset

Straw hats decorated with ribbons and flowers.

Parasol and embroidered bags of that time.

THE AUTHOR: LOUISA MAY ALCOTT

The life of Louisa May Alcott, born in Germantown, Pennsylvania in the United States, is very like the story that made her so famous: **Little Women***.*

Just like Jo, the "little woman" with whom she closely identified, Louisa had three sisters. The Alcott family, just like the Marches in the story, were not very well-off, but not because their father was at war, as happens in the story. Louisa's father taught philosophy and was a man of great ideals, a vegetarian and a supporter of women's right to vote and the abolition of slavery in America. He was very dedicated to fighting for his ideals, but he was not very good at providing for his family.

So from a very early age, Louisa began to earn money by making dolls' clothes. Later on she worked as a seamstress, a teacher and even as a maid.

When the civil war broke out in America, she volunteered as a nurse, but caught typhoid fever and was sent home.

Meanwhile, she also wrote short stories for newspapers, but she only became famous when a publisher asked her to write a novel for girls.

At first she replied, "I don't really like girls very much. I prefer boys." Then she wrote **Little Women** *(1868-69) and became rich and famous. Her first novel was, in fact, followed by many others, including* **An Old-Fashioned Girl** *(1870),* **Little Men** *(1871), and* **Jo's Boys** *(1886), all of which have been very successful. She never married, but, when her sister died young, she brought up her niece as if she were her own daughter.*

To her own family, once so poor, she was able to give comfort and ease thanks to her books, which are read the world over.

CHRISTMAS DAY

"Christmas won't be Christmas without any presents," grumbled Jo.

"It's so dreadful to be poor!" replied Meg.

"And to think that some people have everything..." sighed Amy, the youngest of the four sisters.

"We've got Mother and Father and we've got each other," added Beth.

"We haven't got Father with us now..."

And each of them thought about Father far away at war, for goodness knew how long yet.

Meg, the oldest of the March girls, was sixteen, with large hazel eyes, plenty of curly brown hair and very white hands, of which she was rather proud.

Josephine, or Jo, was fifteen and had that awkward look of someone who had shot up too fast. Her face was lit up by her grey eyes and was surrounded by long, thick hair which she usually wore bundled into a net, to be out of her way.

Beth was fair skinned, with blonde hair and bright, gentle eyes. She was very shy and quiet, but was also kind and courageous.

Amy was the youngest and was blonde with blue eyes. She liked to behave like a lady and was very mindful of her manners.

Their mother would be home soon and the girls set about making the house warm and welcoming.

Jo, who loved to write

poetry, had written a play which the sisters were preparing to put on. She was also directing it and, to her great satisfaction, played all the men's parts too.

They rehearsed until their mother came in. Mrs March was a kindly woman, elegantly dressed, even if her clothes were rather unfashionable.

"Well, dearies, how have you got on today? There was so much to do at the Association for Soldiers' Aid that I couldn't come home for lunch."

She put her slippers on, sat down at the supper table and prepared to enjoy the happiest hour of her busy day, with her four daughters.

"I've got some news for you," she declared. "A letter from your father. He is well and sends his wishes for Christmas and a special message for you girls."

"When will he come home, Marmee?" asked Beth, longingly.

"Certainly not for many months. He will stay and do his work as voluntary chaplain as long as necessary and we mustn't ask him to come back a minute sooner. Now come and hear the letter."

Their father described life in the military camp and only towards the end did his emotion overflow. "Give the girls my love and tell them I think of them constantly. A year seems a long time to wait, but time well spent passes more quickly. I'm sure that when I come back to them, I will find them much improved and may be even prouder of my little women."

"To help you improve yourselves, as Father said, each one of you must look under your pillow on Christmas morning and you will find your guidebook, full of help and suggestions," said Mrs March, "and from this evening, you will each try to behave better."

They all agreed to do as their mother said. That very evening, after supper, they sewed sheets for Aunt March with none of the usual grumbling and divided up their work like a game.

Jo was the first to wake on the grey dawn of Christmas morning. Remembering her mother's promise, she slipped her hand under her pillow and drew out a little crimson-covered bible.

She woke Meg and the others. After wishing each other "Merry Christmas!" they found their copies of the book under the pillow, every one with a different coloured cover.

"Girls," said Meg seriously, "Mother wants us to read these books every day and we must start at once. I shall do so every morning as soon as I wake."

Later on, when they went to thank their mother, they found that she had gone out. Hannah, the house-maid, who was considered more part of the family than a servant, told them that their mother had gone to help some poor folk.

While they waited for their mother to return, they carefully set out the gifts they had bought for her on the table, which

was all ready for Christmas breakfast.

A loud slam of the door told them that Mother was back.

"Merry Christmas, Marmee. Thank you for our books!" they cried in chorus.

"Merry Christmas, little daughters. I want to say something to you before

we sit down. Nearby, there is a poor woman with a little new-born baby and six other young ones and they have no wood and no food. Will you give them your breakfast as a Christmas present? We will make do with bread and milk when we come back."

After a few moments' hesitation, the girls were rushing to gather up the bread and cakes that had been prepared for them and soon set out to the miserable room where the Hummels lived.

It was dark and freezing cold and the six older children were huddled together trying vainly to keep warm, while the baby wailed in its mother's arms.

They handed round their breakfast to these poor people and when they got back home, they had empty stomachs, but their hearts were full of joy.

The afternoon was devoted to the play.

The girls had truly worked miracles. With very little money and a great deal of imagination they had made all of the scenery and wonderful costumes.

Afterwards, a surprise awaited them. Someone had sent them piles of cakes, sweets and biscuits.

"Was it the fairies? Was it Santa Claus? Or was it Aunt March who sent us all these wonderful things?" asked the girls.

"All wrong. Old Mr Laurence sent them," explained Mother. "He heard about what you did this morning and sent you all these things to make up for it."

"It was his nephew who told him," said Jo confidently. "He's a capital fellow and I wish we could get acquainted."

"He is a well-mannered boy, so I have no objection to your knowing him, if a proper opportunity comes along," concluded Mrs March.

AN INVITATION

"Jo, Jo! Where are you?" cried Meg from the foot of the garret stairs, waving a letter. She found her sister buried in a novel, with tears running down her cheeks.

"Look, a proper invitation! 'Mrs Gardiner would be happy to see Miss Meg and Miss Josephine March at a little dance on New Year's Eve.' Marmee says she will let us go. What shall we wear?"

They only had one elegant dress each and Jo had a problem with hers as it was scorched at the back.

"You'll just have to sit all you can and not dance. And remember to behave like a lady. Don't put your hands behind your back, or stare at the other guests."

After much fussing, the girls were ready. Meg wore her silvery grey dress with lace frills and Mother's pearl brooch. She had put her hair up and was wearing very elegant, but very tight, high-heeled dancing slippers.

As for Jo, she looked very pretty in her maroon dress with a white flower as its only decoration, but the nineteen pins holding up her hair were a real torture to her.

THE LAURENCE BOY

On the way, Meg warned her wild sister, "Hold your shoulders straight and don't shake hands if you are introduced to anyone. If you do something wrong, I shall raise my eyebrows, so you'll know."

Mrs Gardiner greeted them kindly and handed them over to Sallie, her eldest daughter. Meg knew Sallie and soon went off with her, leaving Jo alone and feeling out of place.

Things got worse when the dancing started. Fearing someone would ask her to dance, Jo slipped into a curtained alcove, only to find herself face to face with the Laurence boy, who had had the same idea.

"Dear me! I didn't know anyone was here. I don't wish to disturb you," said Jo.

"Don't go away, please! I hid here too because I don't know many people," responded the boy.

They soon made friends. Jo took the opportunity of thanking him for their Christmas present and she begged him to describe his travels in Europe.

Jo took a good look at her new friend. He was a handsome boy of about fifteen, with black hair and black eyes.

Then the young man, whose name was Laurie, asked her to dance.

"I can't," replied Jo, and not knowing what to invent, she told him about her scorched dress.

"Never mind that. There's a long hall out here where we can dance and no one will see us."

In the large empty hall, Laurie taught Jo a new step and they danced for a long time, until they were interrupted by the arrival of Meg, pale and limping from a sprained ankle.

"It aches so. I don't know how I'm ever going to get home."

"Can I help you?" said Laurie, coming back with a cup of coffee and a huge dish of ice-cream. He offered to take the girls home in his carriage.

At home, the girls chattered about the party. They had both had a capital time and Meg had even been invited to spend a week with her friend Annie Moffat's family.

They crept up to bed trying not to disturb anyone, but their two little sisters made them tell all about the party.

The next morning at breakfast, everyone was very cross. It's hard to take up the daily routine again after the Christmas holidays!

Meg and Jo finally set off, carrying the hot turnovers Hannah had prepared for them.

They walked a short way together and Jo, who was always jolly, managed to cheer her sister up a little before they parted, each to face her own day's work.

Some years earlier, when Mr March had lost all his property trying to help an unfortunate friend, the two oldest girls had decided to work to help the family.

Meg had found a place as a nursery governess with the rich King family. It made her feel that she would have liked to be rich and have a wonderful life herself.

Jo happened to suit old Aunt March, who wanted her for a companion part of the day.

Jo had become rather fond of the peppery old lady, and even more so of her large library. The moment she could, Jo curled up in there and devoured entire volumes.

Beth was too bashful to go to school and had done her lessons at home with her father. Even after he had gone away she carried on faithfully by herself. She also helped Hannah with the housework.

She, too, had her troubles to bear. The biggest of these was not having a fine piano to play. Theirs was so old and out of tune!

But Beth played it all the same, accompanying her mother and sisters as they sang and generally living quietly and cheerfully, helping those who needed her.

If anyone had asked Amy what the greatest trial of her life was, she would have answered at once, "My nose."

She insisted that Jo had ruined it by letting her fall when she was a baby, and though it was rather flat, it certainly wasn't cause for such suffering.

Amy had a talent for drawing and devoted many happy hours to it.

The evening, when they sat together sewing, was the time when each of them would tell what they had done during the day.

A NEW FRIENDSHIP

"Where are you going, Jo?" asked Meg, seeing her sister all wrapped up, going out into the snow.

"I'm off to find adventure," said Jo with a

twinkle in her eye.

Meg took up her book again and Jo went off to dig the snow, clearing a path right round the garden to the Laurences' side.

The house where the March family lived was old and brown and covered with ivy, while the stately stone mansion of the Laurences was like an enchanted castle, yet it seemed lonely and sad.

Jo wished to get to know her neighbours more than ever since the party. As she peeped through the hedge she saw old Mr Laurence go out and, looking up at the windows, she thought she saw Laurie. She tossed a snowball up at the window and it opened.

"Are you sick, Laurie?"

"I'm better now, but I've had a bad cold."

"Don't you get bored with no one to keep you company? You must have some friends, but boys make such a row, you need a nice girl."

"But I don't know any."

"You know us... Wait there!" said Jo laughing.

THE DREADED MR LAURENCE

Jo came in a few minutes later holding a covered dish in one hand and three little cats in the other.

Beth had insisted on sending her cats; Jo and Laurie laughed and played with them for a while. Then Jo uncovered the dish which held a lovely piece of cake, and offered to read to Laurie.

Laurie was very interested in his four neighbours. He often watched them, and seeing that peaceful, loving family together made him miss the motherly affection he had never known. When he mentioned it to Jo, she replied, "Instead of peeping at us from afar, why don't you come over and see us? Mother would be very pleased."

Jo told him all about her work and how much she loved books, and Laurie offered to show her those belonging to his grandfather – the dreaded Mr Laurence.

"I'm not afraid of anything, not even him," declared Jo.

Their visit to the library was interrupted by the arrival of the doctor, who

had come to see the boy. Laurie excused himself and asked Jo to wait for
him. She was only too happy to look around at the rich shelves full of books,
coins and other rare objects. She stopped before a portrait of the old man.
"Now I'm sure I shouldn't be afraid of him, despite his grim expression. He
isn't as handsome as my grandfather, but I like him," said Jo, as the door
behind her opened.

"Thank you, ma'am!"

Jo, who had been expecting Laurie, now turned to find herself face to
face with the dreaded Mr Laurence himself, who said, "So, you're not afraid
of me, hey?"

"Not much, sir."

"And I'm not as handsome as your grandfather, but you like me?"

"Yes, sir!"

"You've got your grandfather's spirit. He was a brave and honest man
and I was proud to be his friend."

Then the bell rang for tea and as they went to meet Laurie, Mr Laurence gave Jo his arm. On seeing this, Laurie could hardly conceal his surprise.

After tea, Laurie took Jo to the greenhouse and filled her arms with flowers to take home to her mother.

When they returned to the drawing room, Jo noticed a grand piano in the corner of the room and asked Laurie to play something for her. He did as she asked, but Jo had the impression that the old man was not pleased.

Later, at home, Mrs March told her why old Mr Laurence had seemed so sad. It was because Laurie's mother was an Italian musician, and old Mr Laurence had refused to meet her.

The boy was left all alone when his parents died, and his grand-

father had brought him home, but he did not approve of Laurie's liking for music.

Jo and her family got on very well with Laurie and their new friendship with the Laurences grew steadily.

Mrs March enjoyed talking to old Mr Laurence about her father; Meg adored the conservatory as Jo did the library, Amy never tired of admiring the beautiful paintings and works of art in that house. But the happiest of all was Laurie. In the homely calm of the March family, he had found the joy and happiness of boyhood.

A Pair of Slippers for Mr Laurence

Only Beth did not join in the happy visits. Mr Laurence noticed this and decided to do something about it. So one day, he went round to visit Mrs March.

"You know, Laurie doesn't really play much any more, and the piano suffers now that no one uses it. Would your girls mind coming to practise on it now and then?"

"I'll come, sir," said Beth, turning bright red, "if you are quite sure no one will hear me and be disturbed."

Her eyes shone with happiness and the old man was very touched.

The next day, Beth quietly slipped into the big house and made her way to the piano. There, she found some pretty, easy music which she played happily.

After that, Laurie stood guard in the hall every day so that no one would disturb the little musician. Mr Laurence secretly listened to her play the music and exercises which he put there especially for her.

"I'd like to embroider a pair of slippers for Mr Laurence," said Beth to her mother one day, "but I'm not sure how to do it on my own."

"Don't you worry. I'll get the materials and the girls will help you with the difficult parts."

The slippers were soon finished and, with Laurie's help, they were smuggled on to the desk in the gentleman's study.

Two days later, as Beth was coming back from some errand, she noticed her sisters at the window waving excitedly.

"Come quickly and see what's arrived for you!"

In the parlour stood a little cabinet piano waiting for her, with a letter: *"Dear Madam, I have never had such a beautiful pair of slippers! Allow me to return your kindness by sending you something I hope you will like. With hearty thanks and best wishes!*

James Laurence"

In the excited confusion that followed, Mother said, "You'll have to go and thank him."

"Yes, I mean to!" said Beth and walked deliberately down the garden to the Laurences' house. She walked right into the study and threw her arms round the old gentleman's neck, just like a granddaughter, showing him all her affection.

From that moment, there was a special bond between the old man and Beth.

Amy and Jo

"That boy is a perfect rider, isn't he?" said Meg one day as Laurie came by on horseback.

"But I just wish I had a little of the money he spends on that horse!" said Amy.

"Why might that be?" asked Meg.

"Because I'm dreadfully in debt," replied Amy, explaining that it was the fashion to offer and eat pickled limes at school and that she had received lots but couldn't return the favour because she had no money.

Her sisters kindly gave her a quarter and the next morning, Amy arrived at school happily displaying a moist brown paper parcel with twenty-four delicious limes, which were about to cause her quite some bother.

One of her class-mates was jealous of Amy for the praise she had received from the teacher, Mr Davis, for her beautifully drawn maps. The girl told the teacher about Amy's limes and he was obliged to punish her.

He gave her several strokes of the cane on her palms and made her throw the limes out of the window.

The event changed Amy's life. She was still upset when she got home and told her family what had happened. Mrs March strongly disapproved of corporal punishment and decided that her daughter should study at home in the future.

One Saturday morning, Meg and Jo were getting ready to go out. Amy, who had been kept indoors with a bad cold, insisted on knowing where they were going. dressed up so.

The girls wouldn't give her an answer, but when she noticed their fans, she guessed that they were going to the theatre and threw quite a tantrum because she wanted to go with them.

"You can't come," replied Jo bluntly. "Laurie

only invited us two, so three of us can't turn up!"

And off she went with Meg to meet Laurie who was waiting for them.

Just as the party was setting out, Amy called in a threatening tone, "You are going to be sorry for this, Jo March. See if you aren't."

When she got back, Jo quickly checked her things and seeing that everything was in its place, decided that Amy must have forgotten her revenge.

It wasn't until the following day that she discovered the precious little black book in which she had written all her fairy tales was missing. It didn't take long to find out that Amy had burnt it to spite her.

Jo's hot temper flared and she shouted furiously, "You wicked, wicked girl! I'll never forgive you as long as I live!"

The loss was really very great. The half a dozen fairy tales in the little book represented several years of loving work and the whole family had

secretly hoped that they might be published one day.

The following day, after a most trying morning with Aunt March, Jo decided to go skating on the river with Laurie in the hope that he would pull her out of her bad mood.

Meg advised Amy to follow them and wait until Jo seemed cheered up. Then she should apologise to her sister and try to make it up with her again.

It was the last ice of the season and Laurie told Jo to keep near the banks, as it wasn't safe to skate in the middle.

Amy, who was just coming up behind, didn't hear his warning.

Laurie was already far ahead, but he turned round just in time to see Amy throw up her hands and go down with the sudden crash of broken ice. He immediately rushed back and set about saving her.

Once she had been dragged out of the icy water, the poor thing was

wrapped up as best as possible and taken home. Here, Mother warmed her up and put her to bed. She soon fell asleep while Jo sat watching, her heart bursting with remorse.

She bent down to stroke her little sister's damp head. As if she understood, Amy opened her eyes and held out her arms to Jo and everything was forgiven and forgotten in one big hug.

AN INVITATION TO THE MOFFAT'S

Grand things were afoot for Meg. Annie Moffat had not forgotten her promise and invited Meg to spend two weeks with her. Meg was able to accept the invitation as the King children had the measles.

The travel trunk was dusted off, and her sisters all helped eagerly with the preparations.

The best clothes and accessories were carefully cleaned and brushed and each of the sisters lent the lucky one the newest or prettiest things they had. At last, a very excited Meg set off.

The Moffats were very fashionable. In their splendid house, Meg was pampered and spoilt and it was like living in a fairy-tale, until the evening of the first important party.

The other girls all had splendid dresses, especially bought for the occasion. Meg thought her old dress looked shabbier than ever beside them.

However, the arrival of a huge bouquet of roses raised Meg's status in the eyes of the others. Laurie had sent them. Meg quickly made up some dainty bouquets and shared them among her friends, keeping just a little posy for herself to pin to her belt.

Meg enjoyed herself very much that evening, but she was quickly brought down to earth by a bit of conversation she happened to overhear by chance.

"How old is she?" said one voice.

"Sixteen or seventeen," replied another.

"She would be so nice, poor thing, if she were only dressed more elegantly..."

"That dress is so dowdy. We could offer to lend her one for Thursday, then she won't look so bad... I've invited the Laurence boy, too," said Mrs Moffat.

Over the next few days, she noticed that the other girls often mentioned her friendship with Laurie. She was terribly embarrassed when Mrs Moffat asked what she was going to wear for the ball on Thursday.

"My old white dress again," replied Meg, feeling very uncomfortable.

"Now Meg, please make me happy by letting me dress you up myself," said Belle, the oldest of the Moffat girls. "I have a sweet blue silk you could wear and you'd look a regular beauty."

Meg couldn't refuse the offer, but on Thursday she was hardly recognisable as herself. The blue dress was very tight and very low in the neck, the long skirts tripped her up, although she liked the high-heeled blue silk boots

very much. As she looked at herself in the mirror before going downstairs, she felt like a crow in the borrowed plumes of a peacock.

Despite her discomfort, Meg was excited and happy. But her laughter stopped when she turned to find herself facing Laurie, who was staring at her with undisguised surprise and disapproval.

"I'm glad you came..." she began.

"Jo asked me to come, and tell her how you looked."

"And what will you tell her?" asked Meg, full of curiosity to know his opinion of her.

"I shall say I didn't know you, for you look so unlike yourself, and I don't like you at all. I don't like fuss and feathers," replied Laurie, with none of his usual politeness.

"You are the rudest boy I ever saw," said Meg, petulantly walking away.

Meg was standing alone, still feeling very ruffled, when Laurie, with his very best bow, asked her to dance.

"Please don't tell them at home about my dress tonight," pleaded Meg as they danced. "Mother would only worry. I want to tell them myself how silly I've been."

"I give you my word I won't. I'll just say you looked pretty and were having a good time, even if it isn't true."

"You're right," whispered Meg, "this sort of fun isn't for me."

The following Saturday, when she went home, Meg had had quite enough of parties and fun, and appreciated the simplicity of her life at home all the more.

THE PICKWICK CLUB

Spring had arrived. Gardening, walks and rowing on the river filled the sunny afternoons. And when it rained, other diversions were found, some old, some new.

As secret societies were the fashion, and as all four girls were great admirers of Dickens, they had founded a society and called themselves the "Pickwick Club".

Every Saturday, they met in the garret to read the club's weekly newspaper, to which all contributed something. It was an amusing paper, filled with original tales, poetry and local news.

This particular Saturday evening, when they had finished reading the paper, Jo rose to make a proposition.

"Mr President and gentlemen, I wish to propose the admission of a new member. A worthy and deserving person: Laurie Laurence."

They put the motion to the vote and some were for and some against. But Jo managed to convince the doubtful members, and all voted for.

Then Jo let Laurie out of the closet where he had been hiding, waiting for them to vote.

"As a token of my gratitude, I have set up a post office for the convenience of all club members. It is the old bird house, which I personally have cleaned and repaired so that we can pass letters, books and all sorts of things. Allow me to give you the key."

THE PICNIC

"The first of June! The Kings are off to the seaside tomorrow. I'm free for three lovely months!" exclaimed Meg.

"Aunt March left today too, but I spent the whole day terrified that she would ask me to go with her," said Jo, flopping down on the bed.

"Don't let's do lessons for a while, Beth. Let us have a holiday, too," begged Amy.

After a year's hard work, the girls felt they deserved a complete rest and each wanted to do exactly as she pleased.

"You may try your experiment for a week," agreed Mother, "but I think you'll soon find that all play is as boring as all work."

Each of the girls spent the next day doing exactly as she pleased and that evening they all declared themselves perfectly satisfied.

Nevertheless, the day had, in fact, seemed unusually long to all of them.

As the week crawled on, the girls began to long for it to be over. They had never been so bored in their lives.

Hoping to impress the lesson more deeply, Mrs March decided to finish the week appropriately by giving Hannah a holiday.

When the girls went down for breakfast on Saturday morning, they found no mother, no fire in the kitchen and no breakfast. Mother said she was very tired after a heavy week and had decided to rest quietly in her room that day, and that as she would be going out for lunch later, they could get whatever they liked.

The girls were glad to have something to do at last and did their best. Meg prepared breakfast, but it was so awful that, to comfort her, Jo offered to prepare lunch.

Despite her lack of culinary experience, Jo happily invited Laurie to lunch and trotted off eagerly to do the shopping.

Feeling pleased with herself, she came back from the market with a very young lobster, some very old asparagus and two boxes of unripe strawberries.

On arriving home, she found that she had forgotten to put the bread in the oven and the pastry had soured. Then she found that the water for washing the dishes was cold because the fire was out!

And there, in a corner of the kitchen, was Beth, crying her eyes out over her dead canary.

The meal was a disaster and so was the rest of the day. Mother was right: all play was as bad as all work. "If you do your share of the work, then you'll enjoy your share of play much more," she always said.

One morning in early July, Jo received a letter from Laurie. Some English friends of his, the Vaughns, were visiting and he was going to pitch a tent by the river for a picnic. The girls were all invited. Meg's friend Sallie Gardiner, Ned Moffat and Laurie's tutor John

Brooke would be there, too.

The girls happily agreed, and on the appointed day Laurie introduced them all. Even Beth soon overcame her shyness among these happy friends.

They pushed off in two boats to reach the picnic spot, at Longmeadow. On the way, Meg had a chance to admire the skills of Mr Brooke as he sat

opposite her at the oars. He was a grave, silent young man, with a pleasant voice and handsome brown eyes with which he looked at her a great deal.

At lunch time, Mr Brooke gave them all their tasks and soon a very jolly meal was had by all. After this, they had great fun playing all kinds of games.

Later on, Meg sat down under an oak tree with Kate Vaughn and Mr Brooke.

Kate took out her sketchbook and showed it to Meg, who said admiringly, "How beautifully you draw! I wish I could, but I don't have time."

"Does your schooling take up so much time?"

"I don't study any more, In fact, I am a governess myself," replied Meg, feeling a little embarrassed.

"Oh! Indeed!" said Kate rather disdainfully. Mr Brooke added quickly, "Young ladies in America love independence, and are admired and respected for support-ing themselves."

"Did you like the German song, Miss March?" he asked, turning to Meg to break the silence.

"Oh yes! It was very sweet and I'm much obliged to you for translating it for me."

"Don't you read German?" asked Kate, with a look of surprise.

"Not very well. Since my father went away, I've no one to correct my pronunciation," answered Meg.

"Try a little now. Here's a German book and a tutor who loves to teach," said Mr Brooke.

"It's so hard I'm afraid to try," said Meg.

"I'll read a bit to encourage you," said Kate and read a page in a perfectly correct, but perfectly expressionless manner. Meg's pronunciation was not so perfect, but the soft intonation of her musical voice gave expression to the harsh words.

"Very well indeed!" said Mr Brooke, praising her.

He and Meg carried on talking together, unaware of everything going on around them.

At sunset, everything was packed and the whole party set off down the river again, singing at the tops of their voices.

On the lawn in front of Laurie's house, the party separated with cordial good-nights and good-byes, for the Vaughns were going to Canada.

SECRETS

For some time the pale October sun had been shining weakly through the attic windows, where Jo was busy working in the garret.

She had been scribbling away all afternoon, totally absorbed in her work, until at last she signed her name with a flourish and threw down her pen.

Then she crept downstairs, put on her coat and, climbing out of the window so as not to be seen, went into town.

Once there, she stopped in front of a tall building where she hesitated and then began to walk quickly up and down, stopping three of four times before going in, much to the amusement of a certain young gentleman watching from a building opposite.

Ten minutes later, when Jo came rushing out with a very red face, she found the young gentleman waiting for her.

"What did you come here for?" asked Laurie, the young gentleman in question.

"I didn't want anyone to know...."

"So it's a mystery, then?"

"Perhaps," replied Jo, amused. "And what were you doing, sir, in that billiard saloon?"

"Begging your pardon, ma'am, it wasn't a billiard saloon, but a gymnasium, and I was taking a fencing lesson."

"I'm glad of that. I wouldn't like to think of you wasting your time in such places. Look at Ned Moffat. Mother won't let us have him in the house and if you grow up like him, she won't let us be your friends," remarked Jo.

"Don't worry. I don't mean to be like him. Are you going to deliver lectures all the way home? If you stop, I'll tell you something interesting. It's a secret and if I tell you, you must tell me your secret," demanded Laurie.

"All right. But promise you won't say anything about it at home, and you won't tease me in private," responded Jo.

"Upon my honour. Fire away," said Laurie.

"Well, I've left two stories with a newspaper and I hope they may be published next week. Now it's your turn," said Jo.

"I know where Meg's glove is, the one she lost ages ago," offered Laurie.

"Is that all?" said Jo, looking disappointed.

Then Laurie whispered something in her ear, but her reaction wasn't what he had expected.

"Meg has an admirer? Oh I wish you hadn't told me!" said Jo.

"But I thought you'd be pleased," said Laurie.

"At the idea of anybody coming to take Meg away? No, thank you!"

"You'll change your mind when somebody comes to take you away," Laurie reminded her.

"I'd like to see anyone try it!" cried Jo fiercely.

"So should I!" chuckled Laurie.

Then to shake Jo out of her bad mood, Laurie proposed a race down the hill.

When they reached the bottom, Jo had forgotten her anger. She was panting, with bright eyes, red cheeks and her hair flying around her shoulders.

Two weeks later, Meg was scandalised by the sight of Laurie chasing Jo all over the garden and shouting about a newspaper that had come in the post. Shrieks of laughter were heard from the rose bower, followed by murmuring and a great flapping of newspapers.

Suddenly, Jo bounced in, laid herself on the sofa and pretended to read.

"Have you anything interesting there?" asked Meg.

"Nothing but a story called 'The Rival Painters'. It won't amount to much, I guess."

"Read it out loud, then at least you'll calm down," suggested Amy.

With a loud "A-hem!" Jo started reading.

"Who wrote it?" asked Beth.

Jo stood up, cast away the paper and replied in a solemn voice, "Your sister!"

Meg, Amy and Beth couldn't believe their ears and only the sight of Jo's name actually printed in the paper convinced them.

Jo explained that the story had been published by an editor who was looking for talented new writers whose work he was willing to publish, but he didn't pay beginners.

Mother received the news with great satisfaction. She was very happy and very proud of Jo.

A TELEGRAM

On a dull afternoon in November, the March girls were moaning about their boring work-a-day lives, when Beth announced that Laurie and Marmee were on their way in.

Laurie had come to ask them to go for a drive in the carriage, and the girls were getting ready to go when they heard a sharp ring. A few seconds later Hannah came in with a yellow envelope.

Mrs March tore it open, read it, and dropped back into her chair as pale as death. While Meg and Hannah supported her, Jo read the telegram, which came from the Washington hospital, in a frightened voice.

"Mrs March, your husband is very ill. Come at once."

For some minutes, the room was silent. The girls realised how much their lives could change.

"I shall go at once, but it may be too late. Oh! children, help me to bear it," said Mother, deeply upset.

Everybody was sobbing, even Jo. Poor Hannah was the first to recover. "I won't waste time crying now. I'll go and get your things ready right away, ma'am," she announced.

Laurie promised to protect the girls during their mother's absence, but he seemed far more worried about Mrs March having to face such a journey alone. He left the house, and set off to find a way of solving the problem in some way.

A little later, Meg was rushing around packing, when suddenly Mr Brooke arrived at the front door.

"I am very sorry to hear of this, Miss March," he began quietly, "and as I have various errands to do in Washington, I came to offer myself as escort to your mother."

Towards evening, Jo, who had gone out, still had not come back. Laurie went off to find her, without luck, and Mrs March began to get very anxious.

A while later, however, Jo came walking in with a strange expression on her face. She laid a little roll of bank notes before her mother, saying, "This is to help make father better!"

"Twenty-five dollars! Where did you get it?" asked her mother.

"Don't worry. It's mine, honestly. I only sold what was my own," replied Jo.

As she spoke, Jo took off her bonnet to show her cropped head.

"My dear girl, there was no need for this sacrifice, but I know you did it out of love, and I love

you the more dearly for it," said Mother, deeply touched.

"I wanted to do something for Father. Meg has already given all her salary towards the rent, but I didn't have anything to give. I wandered around for a while and then I saw ponytails of real hair in a barber's window for sale at forty dollars. So I walked straight in, asked them to buy my hair, and I told them why, too," explained Jo.

DEPARTURE

That night in bed, Meg lay awake thinking, when suddenly she realised that Jo was crying.

"Are you crying about Father?" she asked.

"No! I'm crying for my hair. I'm ashamed of myself, but I just couldn't help it. I'm over it now," replied Jo.

The girls woke up at dawn and as they dressed, they agreed to say good-bye cheerfully, so as not to make Mother any more anxious than she was.

Nobody talked much at breakfast, and when the carriage arrived Mrs March whispered in a trembling voice, "Children, I leave you in Hannah's care and Mr Laurence's protection. Don't grieve and fret, but be strong and keep busy." As the carriage rolled away, the little group smiled and waved.

As soon as the girls were back inside, they started to cry. Hannah wisely let them grieve and then, armed with a steaming coffee pot and some kind words, she soon had them feeling better and ready to face their new responsibilities.

Before long, they were cheered by news of their

father. He had been seriously ill, but the treatment was working miracles. The letters from Washington soon became quite reassuring.

The girls wrote long letters to their parents far away, as they had no other way of comforting them.

Even Hannah wrote to reassure them that everything was going first rate. They still had enough money and the girls were behaving well.

Laurie added a few light-hearted words, and a couple of lines from Mr Laurence ended the letter. He gave the parents further assurances and renewed his friendly offers of help.

BETH FALLS ILL

The girls were models of good behaviour for a week, but as the anxiety about their father was relieved, they gradually began to fall back into the old ways. Beth, however, did not forget her duties.

"Meg, I wish you'd go and see the Hummels," she said, about ten days after Mrs March's departure.

"I'm too tired to go today," replied Meg from her comfortable armchair.

"Can't you, Jo?" implored Beth.

"It is too stormy for me with my cold, especially to go to the Hummels," responded Jo.

"You or Hannah ought to go. I've been every day, but now the baby is sick and I don't know what to do for it. My head aches and I'm tired, so I thought maybe one of you could go today," explained Beth.

But later, seeing that nobody else would, Beth put on her hood and trudged off to the poor house. It was late when she came back, upset and worried.

"Jo, the baby died in my arms!"

"What baby?" asked Jo.

"Mrs Hummel's. When I got there she was still out. She had gone to fetch the doctor, but it was too late when he came and he could only say that it had died of scarlet fever."

"You poor dear. How dreadful for you! I ought to have gone!" said Jo,

looking worried.

Beth soon started having the first symptoms of the very contagious fever.

"Don't let Amy come near me. She's never had scarlet fever, and I should hate to give it to her," warned Beth.

It was decided that Amy should be sent to stay with Aunt March, while one of the older girls looked after Beth.

Beth was much sicker than they had suspected. Days passed and there was no sign of her improvement.

There was bad news from Washington, too. Father had had a relapse and would not be coming home for a long time.

The girls did not mention Beth's illness to their parents for now, so as not to worry them unnecessarily. But Beth got worse, her temperature was very high and at times she was delirious. She no longer recognised anyone and when Doctor Bangs came on his daily visit, he advised them to send for Mrs March.

Jo snatched the telegram, which had been ready for days, and rushed out into the driving snow. She was soon back, and Laurie, seeing her tears tried to comfort her. He took her hands in his and, not knowing what to say, simply stroked her head.

It was the best thing he could have done, for the unspoken sympathy and affection Jo felt soon dried her tears and gave her hope and courage.

Laurie slipped away and returned almost immediately with a glass of wine. "Drink it to Beth's health. I telegraphed your mother yesterday and Brooke answered he'd bring her at once, She'll be here tonight."

"Oh Laurie! I'm so glad," laughed Jo, hugging Laurie and giving him two bashful kisses on the cheek.

The news that Mother was coming made everyone feel much better. All day Jo and Meg watched Beth, anxiously waiting for the doctor, who had said he would come around midnight.

The clock struck one and her two sisters were afraid Beth might die before the doctor came.

Suddenly a change took place, Beth's face seemed peaceful.

Hannah, who had fallen asleep on the sofa, started out of her sleep and hurried to the bed. "The fever's turned. She's sleeping naturally and breathes easy!" she whispered.

The doctor arrived just at that moment and confirmed that she had improved greatly. The two girls held each other, with hearts too full for words.

Laurie's joyful voice came from the hall: "Girls, She's here! She's here!"

Words cannot describe the joy of the meeting of the mother and her daughters, and no one was happier than they were in that moment.

When Beth woke from a long, restful sleep, the first thing she saw was her mother's face. She smiled weakly and, nestled in her mother's loving arms, she slept again, still clutching her mother's hand with her own thin one. Mrs March stayed at Beth's side in the big chair all that night and all the next day, while the older girls waited on her and asked for news of Father.

In the evening, Jo went up to Beth's room and approached her mother with a rather worried and undecided look.

"I want to tell you something, Mother. It's about Meg." She began nervously, "It's a little thing, but it bothers me."

"Beth is asleep: speak softly and tell me all about it," responded Marmee.

"Last summer, Meg lost a glove and Mr Brooke has kept it in his pocket. When Laurie found him out, Mr Brooke admitted that he liked Meg, but didn't dare say so."

"Do you think Meg cares for him?" asked Mrs March with an anxious look.

"Oh! I don't know," exclaimed Jo. "She certainly doesn't behave like the silly girls in novels. She eats, drinks and sleeps like a normal person."

"Then you fancy Meg is not interested in John?" said Marmee.

"Who?" cried Jo, staring.

"Mr Brooke. At the hospital he's been so devoted that your father has become very fond of him and fell into the habit of calling him by name. He was perfectly open and honourable about his feelings for Meg, but he wants to speak to her about it only after he has found a good position."

"Oh dear!" muttered Jo. "It's even worse than I imagined. I don't want Meg to leave us, and now she'll go and fall in love and bring an end to all our peace and fun together."

"I want to keep my girls as long as I can, too," sighed Marmee. "It's natural and right that you should all have your own lives, but I won't allow Meg to bind herself in any way while she is too young."

"I'm disappointed! I'd hoped for Meg to marry Laurie and stay near us," said Jo.

"Laurie is too young for Meg, and, in any case, you must leave well enough alone and let time do its work."

FATHER COMES HOME

As Beth and her father both improved rapidly, Mr March began to talk of coming home.

Christmas approached, and the usual mysterious preparations filled the old house. The busiest workers of all were Jo and her friend Laurie.

Christmas Day looked like it would be splendid. Old Mr Laurence had written to say he would be arriv-

ing soon. Beth was uncommonly well and sat at the window to behold her Christmas offering from Jo and Laurie. They had worked by night to build a snowman laden with gifts for their darling Beth.

"I'm so happy!" Beth exclaimed.

"So am I," added Jo, looking at her new books.

"I'm sure I am," echoed Amy, gazing at the picture of the Madonna and Child that Mother had given her.

"Of course I am!" cried Meg, smoothing the folds of her first silk dress, which Mr Laurence had insisted on giving her.

Shortly afterwards, Laurie popped his head in the parlour and said in a peculiar, breathless voice, "Here's another present for the March family."

Before the words were out of his mouth, he disappeared and in his place appeared a tall man muffled up to the eyes, who tried to say something but couldn't.

There was a general stampede and for several minutes Mr March became invisible in the embrace of four pairs of loving arms.

ALL TOGETHER AGAIN

He would never have withstood such an assault had he not been sustained by the arm of Mr Brooke, who had come in with him.

Then the door opened and Beth ran straight

into her father's arms.

Mr Brooke and Laurie withdrew a while, leaving the March family alone to enjoy the happiness of finally being all together again.

Later, Mr March enjoyed Christmas dinner with all the people who had been close to him and his family through the times of sorrow and anxiety.

KIND WORDS FROM MR MARCH

That evening, the happy family sat together round the fire. "It's been a hard time, but I know you have got on bravely," said Mr March.

"How do you know? Did Mother tell you?" asked Jo.

"No, but I've made several discoveries today. Meg's red, roughened hands, so different from the smooth white hands she once had, tell me that she has been very industrious." At these words, Meg smiled happily.

"My wild tomboy daughter has become a neat young lady. I know she watched over Beth when she was ill and cared for her, and this tells me she has become a gentle, tender woman." Jo's eyes were bright with tears.

"As for this little one here, I'm just so glad that I've got you safe. I'm afraid to say much more." And Mr March pressed his cheek against Beth's, gaunt from her recent illness.

"I see that Amy no longer bosses her sisters and she ran errands for her mother all afternoon, so I think she has learned to think of other people more, and less of herself."

The girls stared into the fire, listening to their father's voice. After a while, Beth said, "It's singing time now."

So, sitting at her piano, her sweet voice led them all in song.

The following afternoon, Laurie walked past the window. As he caught sight of Meg sewing, Jo saw him drop down on one knee, beat his breast, tear his hair and clasp his hands imploringly. She could no longer stop herself and said, "That's how your John will be going on by and by. If only he would make up his mind to speak to you! I hate to wait, and for things to be undecided."

"Nothing is undecided because nothing is going to happen. He won't speak to me because Father has told him I'm too young," replied Meg.

"If he did speak, you would not know what to say. You should give him a good, decided 'No!'."

"I'm not so silly and weak as you think. I know exactly what I'd say," responded Meg.

"Would you mind telling me?" asked Jo, full of curiosity.

"I should calmly and decidedly say, 'Thank you, Mr Brooke, you are very kind, but I agree with Father. I am too young to be engaged, but let us be friends as we were.'"

A noise in the hall interrupted them and Meg blushed red as Jo opened the door.

"Good afternoon. I came to get my umbrella, that is, to see how your father is today," said Mr Brooke, getting mixed up with embarrassment.

"It's very well, and he's in the rack. I'll get him and tell it you're here," replied Meg, getting just as embarrassed.

She sidled towards the door with the excuse of going to tell her mother, but John stopped her with a question.

"Are you afraid of me, Meg?" he asked.

"How could I be afraid of you after you've been so kind to Father. I only wish I could thank you for it," replied Meg.

"You don't have to thank me. Just tell me if you care for me a little, Margaret. I love you so much," and the look in his eyes made her forget every word of the speech she had prepared.

"I don't know," she replied softly.

"I need to know how you feel, for I can't work towards the future unless I know," he explained.

"I'm too young..." replied Meg.

"I'll wait, if you will only learn to love me. Would it be a very hard lesson, dear?" asked John.

"Not if I choose to learn it, but..." faltered Meg, with a fluttering heart.

But when she saw the satisfied expression in his eyes, she became capricious and said petulantly, "I don't choose to learn it. Please go away and let me be!"

This change in Meg's mood rather bewildered the young man, "Do you really mean that? Can I hope you'll change your mind by and by?"

Just at that moment, the door opened and Aunt March hobbled in.

"What a surprise to see you, Aunt! We were merely talking..." Meg tried to explain hurriedly, while Brooke vanished into the study.

"Ah! I understand now. You don't mean to marry him, do you? He hasn't got a penny. And if you do, not one penny of my money will ever go to you."

Roused by Aunt March's threats, Meg resolutely declared, "I shall marry whom I please and you can leave your money to anyone you like."

Aunt March saw that she had begun wrong and, after a little pause, made a fresh start, saying as mildly as she could, "Now Meg, my dear, be reasonable. Don't spoil your whole life by making a mistake in the beginning. It's your duty to make a rich match and help your family."

"Father and Mother don't think that," said Meg.

"This chap is poor and he hasn't any work, has he?" inquired Aunt March.

"No, but he has many friends and Mr Laurence is going to help him,"

explained Meg.

"James Laurence is a crotchety old fellow and not to be depended on. If you marry without money, position or business, you'll have to work harder all your life than you do now," said Aunt March.

"I couldn't choose better than John. He is energetic and brave, he's willing to work hard and everyone likes and respects him," responded Meg.

"Well, I wash my hands of the whole affair! Don't expect anything from me when you are married!" and with that the old lady left the house.

Meg, left alone, felt a pair of arms encircling her. Mr Brooke whispered in her ear, "I couldn't help hearing, Meg. Thank you for defending me and proving that you do care for me a little bit."

"I didn't know how much, until she abused you so," murmured Meg.

Fifteen minutes later, Jo came downstairs, thinking that Meg had settled the matter with her speech. However, she was dismayed at the sight of the enemy sitting on the sofa, talking tenderly to her sister.

She rushed upstairs, but Mr and Mrs March hurried down to congratulate the happy couple and there was nothing left for Jo to do but to take refuge in the garret.

Jo waited eagerly for Laurie, for she thought he at least would understand how awful it was, but she was mistaken. Laurie came in bearing a great bridal-looking bouquet for "Mrs John Brooke".

"I knew Brooke would have it his own way. When he makes up his mind, he can accomplish anything!" announced Laurie.

"Thank you. I'll take that as a good omen and invite you to my wedding on the spot," answered Mr Brooke.

"I'll come if I'm at the ends of the earth, if only to console Jo for her loss," and he went to join Jo in a corner.

"You can't know how hard it is for me to lose Meg. She's my dearest friend," explained Jo.

"You've got me! I'm not good for much, but I'll always stand by you, Jo, all the days of my life. And I'll be through college by then and we can go abroad somewhere together," said Laurie.

"That would be wonderful!" sighed Jo, looking around her.

Mother and Father sat together reliving the first chapter of the romance which for them began some twenty years ago.

Amy was drawing the lovers who sat apart in a world of their own.

Beth was lying on the sofa, chatting merrily to Mr Laurence, who held her little hand.

Jo sat down in her favourite seat, and Laurie, leaning on the back of the chair, gave her his friendliest smile.

And so Meg, Jo, Beth and Amy, the four "little women" of the March family, ended their year happily.

THE END

Published by André Deutsch Classics
André Deutsch Ltd
106 Great Russell Street
London WC1B 3LJ
England

© 1992 Dami Editore, Milan
© 1997André Deutsch

Illustrations by Giuseppi Bartoli
Adaption of text by Maria Danesi with additional adaptation by Anna Casalis

ISBN 0 233 99123 9   Printed in Italy